Contents

Introduction

Jane Tennison wanted to shout with anger. For eighteen months she had waited for a murder case but every time something happened, every time there was a murder case, it was given to one of the male officers. Murders were 'man's work', it seemed.

When a young woman is found horribly murdered, Detective Chief Inspector Jane Tennison at last gets the chance she needs to prove herself.

Before long she realises that she is looking for a murderer who has killed before – and will kill again. She must work fast to catch the murderer before he strikes again. But this is only one half of Jane Tennison's battle – she must also fight to win the respect of the men she commands.

And the men are watching her, every step of the way, hoping she'll fail. She must make no mistakes.

Then a second body is found . . .

Lynda La Plante's crime stories and TV films have made her one of Britain's most successful writers. She was born in 1946 in Liverpool, England, and was an actress on TV and in the theatre before she became a writer. Her first TV series, *Widows*, was shown in twenty-six countries and her first novel, *The Legacy*, was an international bestseller.

She spends months or even years finding out about a subject before she writes about it, and sometimes puts herself in dangerous situations to do so. 'People say my characters are very real – that's because they *are* real,' she says.

Prime Suspect is the first of several stories about Detective Chief Inspector Jane Tennison. All the stories were very successful TV films.

Chapter 1   The First Body

Mrs Corinna Salbanna opened her eyes and looked at the clock when she heard the noise. It was almost 2 a.m. Angrily she went downstairs. As she passed Della Mornay's room, she noticed the light was on.

'That woman!' she thought. 'She owes me rent. She brings men back to her room. Now she leaves the front door open in the middle of the night.'

She knocked hard on Della's door.

'Come on! Open it!' she shouted. 'I know you're in there.'

There was no reply. She pushed the door open.

Della's room was as old and dirty as the other apartments in the house. It was untidy, clothes all over the place, and it smelled of cheap make-up. Blankets lay on the floor next to the bed.

'Come out of there right now!' Mrs Salbanna cried. 'I want to speak to you!'

She pulled back one of the blankets.

She opened her mouth to scream, but no sound came.

◆

Chief Detective Officer John Shefford was the last person to arrive at the house. Two police cars and an ambulance were already there. A group of curious neighbours stood near the gate.

The policemen stood back when Shefford walked into the house. They all knew and respected him.

At the bottom of the stairs, he stopped for a moment. He had investigated many murders 'in his time' but this one was different. He forced himself to go upstairs.

Detective Officer Bill Otley was waiting for him.

'It's Della Mornay, boss,' he said quietly.

Inside the room the police doctor was examining the body and speaking into a tape machine.

'She's lying on her face. Her hands are tied behind her back . . .' The doctor waved at Shefford and continued, '. . . a lot of blood on her head and face, serious injuries to her shoulders and chest. She probably died about 12.30 a.m.'

The doctor turned the body over. Shefford turned away; he could not look at her. She had been pretty; now her face was destroyed. Her hair was covered in blood. One eye was completely gone.

'Her name's Della Mornay,' Shefford said. 'She's a prostitute. I've seen her before.'

There was a small book lying under the bed. The doctor did not notice when Shefford picked it up and gave it to Otley without a word.

Otley put the book in his pocket. He would do anything for Shefford. Seven years ago, when Otley's wife died, Shefford was the only person who understood his anger and sadness. Shefford was at the hospital the night Ellen died. He did everything he could to help. He was always there when Otley needed him and, in the months after Ellen's death, Otley spent a lot of time with Shefford and his family. Shefford was his friend as well as his boss. He loved the man, admired him. Otley would do anything for him.

All morning the investigation continued. The doctor continued to examine the body.

'She was killed with a small sharp object, maybe a tool. She had sex with someone before she died. We can do DNA tests to find the blood type of the person who killed her. And something else – there are marks on her arms and wrists. She was tied . . .'

*Shefford turned away; he could not look at her. She had been pretty;
now her face was destroyed.*

Policemen searched Della's apartment. The murderer had not stolen anything – her jewellery and money were still there.

All the prostitutes and call girls who knew Della were interviewed. No luck. Nobody had seen her for many weeks. They thought perhaps she had gone north to visit a friend, but they did not say who.

At 11 a.m., Chief Detective Officer Jane Tennison parked her car outside the police station. It was a cold clear day and she hurried to her office. For three months she had worked on a financial case and she was bored. She had moved to this police department to work on interesting cases, not to sit at a desk all day.

'Why's Shefford here?' she asked Police Officer Maureen Havers.

'He's got a new investigation. A prostitute was murdered last night in Milner Road.'

'How did Shefford get the case?' Tennison asked angrily. 'I thought he was on holiday. I was here until after ten last night.'

Maureen shook her head. 'I don't know.'

Tennison wanted to shout with anger. For eighteen months she had waited for a murder case but every time something happened, every time there was a murder case, it was given to one of the male officers. Murders were 'man's work', it seemed. She stormed out and banged the door behind her.

Shefford received the message on his car radio that evening. DNA tests showed that Della Mornay had had sex with the same man who had attacked a woman in 1988.

'George Arthur Marlow. In prison for eighteen months although he said he wasn't guilty, said he didn't even know the victim. He has the same DNA as the man who murdered Della, no question about it. He's our prime suspect all right.'

4

Shefford drove straight back to the station to pick up the papers he needed to arrest Marlow.

'Right,' he said, putting on his coat again. 'Let's go and get him.'

◆

Jane Tennison opened the door of the small apartment she shared with her boyfriend, Peter Rawlings. They had lived together for three months now. Peter came out of the kitchen and smiled at her. 'Bad day?' he asked. She nodded, walked through to the bedroom and threw her coat on the bed. 'Want to talk about it?' Peter asked.

'Later,' she said. 'Let me have a bath first.'

Jane and Peter had been friends for a long time before they started living together. Peter had been married and had a young son, Joey. When his marriage ended, he spent a long time talking to Jane about what had gone wrong. Over the months they saw each other nearly every day and grew closer until Jane suggested that Peter moved into her flat.

Later, when they were eating dinner, she told him about her problems at the police station. He was a good listener, caring and thoughtful. She had become very fond of him, she realised with surprise. She told him about the way Shefford and the other men did not respect her.

'They think I'm a joke,' she said angrily. 'My boss won't let me work on murder investigations. He tells me to be patient.'

Peter touched her hand. 'You'll get something soon.'

◆

Shefford stood at the door of George Marlow's house. Marlow seemed amazed by the arrival of the police. He stood there holding his cup of coffee, unable to understand what they wanted.

'I'm arresting you as a murder suspect.'

Moyra, Marlow's wife, came out. 'What do you want? Where are you taking him?' she screamed. 'He hasn't had his dinner . . .'

The policemen did not reply. They led Marlow out to the police car. Two officers began to search the house from top to bottom, looking for something that would prove that Marlow had killed Della Mornay.

Moyra watched them; her eyes were cold and hard. She hated policemen, hated them.

♦

Jane lay in bed next to Peter.

'So what will you do?' he asked.

'I'm not leaving. They may want me to leave, but I won't. One day I'll get a murder case and then I'll show them how good I am . . .'

Peter sighed. Jane thought about her work all the time. It was the only thing she talked about.

♦

At the police station George Marlow was quiet but helpful. He asked to telephone his lawyer.

Shefford prepared to question him.

'OK, I'm ready. I know he's the killer,' he told Otley. 'Let's get in there and make him admit it.'

He kicked open the door and walked into the room where Marlow was waiting, his hands on his knees and his head down. Marlow looked up, surprised.

'George? I'm Chief Detective Officer John Shefford and this is Detective Officer Bill Otley. We want to ask you a few questions before your lawyer gets here, OK?'

He smiled and offered Marlow a cigarette. 'You smoke, George?'

'No, sir.'

'Good. Right . . . can you tell me where you were on the night of January 13th? Take your time.'

'January 13th? Saturday? That's easy. I was at home with Moyra. We watched television. Yeah, I was with my wife.'

'Where were you at about ten o'clock?'

'I was at home. Oh no — no, wait a minute. I wasn't at home.'

'Going to tell me where you were, then, George?'

Marlow smiled. 'I went out for a while. I met a girl. You know, a prostitute.'

'Met her before, had you?'

Marlow shook his head. 'No, it was the first time I'd seen her. She was outside the train station at Ladbroke Grove. I stopped and asked her how much.'

'But you're sure you hadn't seen her before? Della Mornay?'

'Della Mornay? Who's Della Mornay?' asked Marlow.

Chapter 2   Interviews

The interview continued throughout the day.

'After we had sex, I took her back to Ladbroke Grove and paid her,' Marlow said. 'The last time I saw her, she was looking into another car, a red . . . maybe a Scirocco . . . I'm not sure what type it was. I thought she'd found another customer.'

'And then what did you do, George?'

'I went home.'

'What time was that?'

'I can't remember. Ask Moyra.'

'Did you know the girl?'

'I'd never seen her before. Like I said, she just came over to my car.'

Shefford showed him a photograph of Della Mornay.

'Come on, George.' Shefford was impatient. 'Was this the girl?'

'I can't remember. It was dark . . .'

In another room, Moyra was asked the same questions again and again. What time did Marlow come home? Did he go out again? She gave the same answers every time. Marlow came home at 10.30. They watched television and went to bed.

When the police let her go, Detective Officer Burkin was sent back to the house with her. He had orders to collect Marlow's car, a brown Mark III Rover. He took two officers with him and they drove Moyra home.

There was no sign of the Rover. It was not parked on the street near the house.

'Someone has probably stolen it,' Moyra said. 'I wouldn't be surprised if you took it yourselves!'

It was 11.30 p.m. when Shefford stopped asking Marlow questions. He had twenty-four hours to find evidence that connected Marlow with the murder. If he couldn't find a link, he would have to let Marlow go home.

'Find Marlow's car,' he told Burkin. 'I want to search it.'

Next morning, Shefford sat at his desk looking through the notes on the case. Otley brought him a cup of coffee.

'Did Burkin find the car?'

'No,' Otley said. 'It isn't parked near the house. Moyra says it must have been stolen.'

'Find it. And Otley, check something for me, will you? There was a girl murdered in Oldham when I worked there. Bring me the information on her.'

'Do you think Marlow murdered her as well?'

'Maybe. I want to check it out.'

Otley pulled Della Mornay's diary out of his pocket. 'What shall I do with this?'

'Keep it. I'll look through it later. I'm going to see the boss and tell him what has happened.'

Jane Tennison arrived at work soon after Shefford. His car was badly parked so it was difficult to find space for her own car next to it.

As she walked into the office, she saw Otley.

'I hear you've got a suspect,' she said.

'Yeah. We arrested him yesterday. His DNA matches the killer's.' Otley spoke sharply to Tennison. Like his boss, he did not enjoy talking to her. He hated ambitious women.

Later that morning, Tennison went to see her boss, Chief Inspector Kernan, to complain about the murder cases always being passed to male officers.

'If you're unhappy at this police station, you can move to another one,' Kernan said.

'I don't want to move. I want to know why Shefford got this case when he was on holiday!'

'He knew the victim.'

'So did I! I knew the victim!' Tennison shouted. 'I arrested her two years ago.'

Kernan told her again that she must be patient.

He was pleased when she left his office. She was a good officer, but she was a woman and he did not like working with women. He, like Shefford and Otley, believed that crime investigation was better done by men. He would be happy when she left the station and went elsewhere.

Later, Shefford also went to see Kernan.

'It looks good, John,' Kernan said. 'Are you OK? You don't look too good.'

'Just tired,' Shefford replied. 'We've been working on this case all day and all night. We need more evidence but there's blood on Marlow's coat. If that matches Della's blood type, we've got him!'

As he spoke, Shefford felt a strong pain in his chest.

Kernan looked at him. 'What's the matter?'

'I don't know. I've got – a – pain –'

Shefford couldn't breathe. The pain got worse. Suddenly he fell, hitting his head on the corner of Kernan's desk.

Kernan telephoned for a doctor. Otley tried to help his boss stand up, but Shefford could not move. His eyes were closed.

Tennison heard somebody shouting outside her office. A doctor ran past.

'What is it?' she asked.

'Shefford's ill.'

Shefford's heart failed and he died before the ambulance reached the hospital.

Tennison sat in her office. She did not like Shefford but she was sorry he was dead. And now somebody else would have to lead the Della Mornay case.

Kernan called his boss, Geoff Trayner, to discuss the situation. Somebody must take over the Della Mornay case and although neither man liked Tennison they knew she was waiting.

'The men won't want to work for her,' Kernan said, 'but who else can we use? None of the other senior officers are available.'

'Right. Put her in charge of the case,' Trayner said, 'but watch her carefully. If she does anything wrong, we'll get rid of her.'

Chapter 3   Tennison Takes Over

Otley was the last person to arrive at the meeting. All the police officers in the room were silent. They had admired their boss and now Shefford was dead. Kernan stood up and began to speak. 'I've looked at the Marlow case and I think we can charge him with Della Mornay's murder. I'm bringing in another senior officer to take over the case. You all know Chief Detective Tennison . . .' There was a shout of protest from the men. Otley stepped forward. 'I'm sorry sir, but you can't let her take over. We don't want her! We've worked as a team for five years. Bring in someone we know.'

'She's the only officer available,' Kernan said, 'and she's taking over the case. There's nothing more to discuss.'

He left the room quickly before there were any more protests. Tennison was going to have trouble working with these men.

Otley emptied everything out of John Shefford's desk. His eyes filled with tears as he looked at the photographs of Shefford's family. He was still sitting at the desk when Burkin came in.

'Tennison's checking through the evidence. Do you want to speak to her?'

'I don't even want to be in the same room as her,' Otley said.

Tennison read all the reports on the Della Mornay case, then she and Detective Jones went to see Mrs Salbanna at the house in Milner Road. The woman couldn't tell her anything.

'She didn't pay her rent,' she complained. 'When will you police finish looking at her room? I could rent it to someone else. I need the money.'

'You saw the body,' Tennison said. 'Are you certain it was Della Mornay?'

'Who else could it be?' Mrs Salbanna asked.

'How well did you know Della?'

'I didn't *know* her, I rented a room to her. I didn't see her often, only when I collected the rent. And she was always late paying that . . .'

11

Tennison looked around Della's room. There were still some clothes and shoes in the cupboard. She looked carefully at the shoes.

Next, Tennison went to look at Della Mornay's body. Someone had cleaned her and combed her hair but the deep cuts on her face were still there. Tennison looked at the marks on Della's arms.

'She was tied by the top of her arms and her wrists,' the doctor said. 'And there's a small cut on her hand.'

'Where?'

The doctor showed her a small cut on the girl's wrist. 'It was quite deep, so it must have bled a lot.'

Tennison nodded and turned to Jones.

'We arrested Della before so we must have a copy of her fingerprints. Check them with the fingerprints from the body.'

'We've already done that,' Jones said.

'Well, do it again. Now.'

♦

That night, as Peter watched television, Jane Tennison continued reading her notes on the case. She looked very tired.

'Come to bed, Jane,' Peter said.

'Soon. I want to finish this.'

Peter went to bed. Jane did not come with him. She worked all through the night and fell asleep sitting at her desk.

At nine o'clock when Tennison entered the meeting room, all the officers were silent. They didn't try to hide how much they disliked her.

'You know that I am now in charge of this case. I'm sorry about Shefford – I know you are upset and shocked by his death. I hope that you'll co-operate with me to close the case.'

She looked at their faces. 'If any of you don't want to work with me, then you can move to another case.'

None of the men spoke. Otley looked at her with hatred.

'OK. Now here's the bad news,' she continued. 'This is a photograph of Della Mornay and this is a photograph of the murder victim. Their fingerprints are not the same. Their feet are different sizes. Our victim is *not* Della Mornay. Somebody made a mistake.'

'You know Shefford identified her,' Otley shouted.

'Then he was wrong. I want to know how Marlow knew her name. At the beginning of his first interview, he said he didn't know the girl. By the end of the second interview, he was calling her Della! How did he find out her name?'

Otley opened his mouth to interrupt but she did not notice him.

'We have to start again. We have to find out who the dead girl is and where Della Mornay is. I think Marlow is involved in this case, but if we don't find more evidence, we can't charge him. So we need to work quickly.'

Nobody spoke as she walked to the door, but when she left the room, all the men started talking.

'I hate her,' Otley said. 'John Shefford only died yesterday and she's trying to make him look like a fool.'

When Tennison went to interview Marlow, she was surprised by how handsome he was. Handsome, polite, wearing an expensive suit.

She introduced herself. 'You know what happened to John Shefford. I'm Chief Detective Tennison. I am now in charge of this case. I need to ask you some more questions.'

Marlow repeated his story. He saw the girl near the station and offered her money to have sex with him.

'And you're sure you'd never seen her before?'

'Which girl?'

'Della Mornay.'

'You knew her then, did you?'

'No, I didn't know her name. I'd never seen her before. Mr Shefford told me her name.'

'OK. Then what happened?'

'We had sex, in the back seat of my car. When she climbed out of the car, she cut her hand on the edge of the radio. I gave her my handkerchief to wrap around her hand because there was blood on her fingers. Then I took her back to the station. She got out of my car and went to another car – a red one. I suppose she found another customer.'

'And you're sure you'd never seen her before?'

'No, and I wish I hadn't seen her then. I was so stupid.'

Otley knocked on the door and Tennison went outside to speak to him.

'We've found some blood on his coat. It's the same type as the victim's. We've got him!'

'No we haven't,' Tennison replied. 'He says that the girl cut her hand in his car – that explains the blood. And Shefford told him Della's name. We haven't enough evidence to prove that he did the murder. If we went to court with this case they would find him not guilty immediately.'

Tennison interviewed Marlow for another hour. Finally she collected her papers together.

'Just one more question, Mr Marlow. You drove home. Is that right?'

'Yes.'

'Do you have a garage?'

'No, I left the car outside the house. The police say they can't find it. Do you think it's been stolen?'

Tennison did not reply. She was walking to the door when Marlow stopped her.

'Excuse me. Can I go home now?'

'No. I'm sorry, Mr Marlow, but you can't.'

♦

Otley was sitting in the meeting room talking to Burkin when Tennison walked in with a big, dark-haired man.

'This is Detective Tony Muddyman. He starts work with us tomorrow. I've told him something about the case, but you can tell him the details.'

Muddyman knew some of the officers and they greeted him. Otley was not sure about him. He did not want any friends of Tennison's working on the team.

Tennison picked up a piece of paper from Otley's desk.

'Are these the names of girls who've been reported missing?'

'Yeah. It says Missing Persons Report on the top of it.'

'Cut it out, Otley,' Tennison said sharply. She looked at the list. 'One in Brighton, one in Surrey, one here in London . . . I'll visit them.'

She reached for the telephone as it rang. It was Peter. She turned away from the men in the room as she talked to him.

'I'm sorry, I can't talk now. Is it important?'

Burkin came into the room looking for her.

'We're ready to search Marlow's house again,' he said.

Tennison promised to call Peter back later. She put the telephone down and went to join Burkin. 'We're looking for a handkerchief,' she said. 'One with blood on it.'

♦

Tennison and Burkin knocked on the door of Marlow's house. They waited a long time before the door was pulled open. Moyra Henson stood there. Tennison looked carefully at her. It was the first time she had seen Marlow's wife. She knew Moyra was thirty-eight but she looked older. She wore expensive clothes and a lot of make-up.

'Yes?' she asked.

'I'm Chief Detective Tennison . . .'

'So what?'

Tennison noted the good jewellery which Moyra wore, expensive bracelets, lots of rings . . . her nails were long and red.

'We want to search this house. We have the necessary papers. I'd like to ask you a few questions while Detective Burkin looks around.'

'I don't have much choice, do I?' Moyra said as she let them in.

The house was tidy and well decorated.

'This is very nice,' Tennison said.

'What did you expect? George works hard, he earns plenty of money. Have you found his car yet? It's your fault it's gone. Somebody will have seen you take him away and stolen the car.'

'I can't give you any information about the car. I just want to have a chat with you. I've taken over the investigation. The other inspector died suddenly.'

'Good! The fewer police, the better!'

'How do you feel about your husband picking up a prostitute, Moyra?' Tennison asked.

'Wonderful! How do you think I feel?'

'What about the girl he attacked before he went to prison?'

'He didn't do anything. That woman was crazy. Maybe George had too much to drink, but he didn't attack her.'

'Was he drunk when he came home on Saturday night?'

'No, he was not!'

'And what time did he arrive home?'

'Half past ten. We watched television and we went to bed.'

Tennison took a photograph from her bag and showed it

to Moyra. 'This is the girl he admits he had sex with. Look at her.'

'So what? I'm sorry the girl's dead but what do expect me to do about it? Plenty of men have sex with other women.'

'One more question, Moyra. Did you know Della Mornay?'

'I've never heard of her.'

'Never?'

'No.'

'And you're certain George didn't know her?'

Moyra folded her arms across her chest. 'I've never heard of her.'

Tennison put the photograph back in her bag. 'Thank you for your time,' she said.

As they left the house, Burkin told her that he had not found any handkerchief with blood on it.

Otley and Jones searched through a list of all the girls who had been reported missing in London during the last month, then they began visiting their homes. One of them could be the murder victim. The first apartment they visited was in a good neighbourhood but the apartment itself was untidy and dirty.

A tall blonde haired girl opened the door.

'My friend, Karen, has been missing for about two weeks. Nobody has seen her. I thought she was staying with her boyfriend, but she isn't.'

'Do you have a photograph of her?' Otley asked.

When he looked at the photograph of the pretty young girl he knew immediately he had found the name of the murder victim.

Tennison and Burkin visited two other families who had reported missing daughters. Neither of them was anything like the murdered girl.

'Otley has done this on purpose. He knew these couldn't be the girls. He's trying to make me look stupid,' she thought.

As they drove back to London, Tennison asked Burkin, 'What do you think of Marlow?'

Burkin answered slowly. 'I think he did it. There's something about him. I don't know what, but I think he's our man.'

Tennison stared out of the car window, talking more to herself than to Burkin. 'You know, being a woman in my position isn't easy. I have feelings about people, but they're probably different to yours. As a man, you feel that Marlow did it. Why? Why do you think it's him?'

'He had sex with her. We know that.'

'That doesn't make him the murderer. We have to find the links, the connections. His wife supports him. He's been in trouble before, but she still supports him.'

'I still think it's him,' Burkin said.

'You can't charge a man because you *think* he's guilty. You have to have evidence.'

At that moment, a message came over the radio. The officers had searched every inch of Della's flat. There was no evidence to show that Marlow had ever been there, not a single hair.

Tennison leaned back in her seat. 'How did he get in there and walk away without leaving anything behind?'

The third house they visited belonged to a rich family. The door was opened by a man.

'Major Howard? I'm Chief Detective Tennison and this is Detective Burkin. We want to ask you some questions about your daughter.'

He let them into the house. 'Of course. Do come in.'

He led them into a large room with big windows which looked out onto the garden.

The elderly man turned to them. 'Please sit down. What can I do for you? Is something wrong?'

'We're looking for your daughter. Nobody has seen her for two weeks.'

'What? Is this a joke?' The man looked upset, but Tennison kept on questioning him.

'Do you have a photograph of your daughter?'

When the Major showed her a photograph, Tennison knew immediately who it was.

'I'm sorry, sir,' she said. 'I have to tell you that I think your daughter is dead.'

Otley and Jones spent the rest of the afternoon interviewing prostitutes. None of them could remember when they last saw Della.

'These women make me angry,' Otley said. 'We should get rid of them all. They'll do anything for money.'

Jones did not reply.

'My wife,' Otley went on, 'was a good woman. She never hurt anybody and she died. Why did she have to die? Why not one of these women?'

Tennison led Major Howard into the room where the body was lying.

'Are you ready?' she asked him.

He nodded.

She pulled back the blanket which covered the body.

'Major Howard, is this your daughter, Karen Julia Howard?'

He stared at the dead girl. Tennison waited. After a long time, he nodded. 'Yes, this is my daughter.'

There were many questions which Tennison wanted to ask him, but he spoke first.

'How did she die? How long has she been here? Why wasn't I told before? Who is in charge of this investigation?'

Tennison interrupted. 'I'm in charge.'

'You? Let me speak to Commander Trayner. He's a friend of

mine. I will not have a woman in charge! Let me see the Commander.'

Tennison opened her mouth to reply but Burkin stopped her.

'Leave him alone,' he said. 'He's upset.'

'I have many friends,' the Major shouted. 'I know many people who could lead this investigation –'

Then he began to cry like a small child.

Tennison was ashamed of herself for wanting to question him. She left the Major and Burkin together. The young police officer put his arm across the older man's shoulders as he kept on crying.

Chapter 4   Another Murder

Next morning, Kernan had three visitors. The first was Tennison with a report that the murder victim had been identified. Second was Otley, complaining that Tennison was a bad police officer.

'We should have charged Marlow with the murder. We have the results of the DNA tests. We know he did it. She's no good.'

The third visitor was Arnold Upcher, Marlow's lawyer.

'I think you should look at these cases, Chief Superintendent. In each one, the evidence depended on DNA tests and in each one the accused was found not guilty. Mr Marlow has said he was at home when the girl was murdered and you don't have enough evidence to prove he committed the murder. You have to let him go.'

♦

Tennison interviewed the girl who lived with Karen.

'The last time I saw her, she was going to work. She was a fashion model. She was always so happy.' The girl burst into tears.

Michael, Karen's boyfriend, could not help.

'We argued. I haven't seen her for a few weeks. I was on holiday until the 13th of January. When I came home I telephoned the apartment and her friend said she wasn't there. Then I telephoned her parents' house but they hadn't seen her since Christmas. So I went to the police and reported that she was missing.'

'Where were you on the night of the thirteenth?'

'At my parents' home. They'll tell you I was there all night.'

♦

At 6.15 p.m., Kernan said they must let Marlow go home. There was not enough evidence to prove that he murdered Karen and the police had kept him as long as they could.

Tennison broke the news to the other police officers.

'We keep investigating him until we find the evidence.'

'You shouldn't have let him go!' Otley shouted. 'If Marlow kills another girl, it will be your fault.'

'That's enough, Sergeant Otley,' Tennison said. 'This case was handled badly from the beginning. There is not enough evidence to charge him, so we will keep searching for more until we can bring him back and keep him here.'

Tennison opened her car door. Marlow ran up to her.

'Excuse me, Miss,' he said. 'I wanted to thank you. I knew you would help me.' Tennison stared at him. He was handsome, he looked innocent, but she knew that he was the murderer. She was certain that he was involved. Marlow got into a taxi. A moment later, Otley ran up to Tennison's car. 'I've just had a telephone call. They've found another body. She was attacked and her hands were tied. From the description, it's Della Mornay.'

It was after 8 p.m. when Tennison and Otley reached the field

Otley ran up to Tennison's car. 'I've just had a telephone call.
They've found another body.'

where the body lay. It was raining hard and the ground was muddy.

The body was covered with dirt. It had been there for a long time. Tennison looked at the face.

'I think you're right. It looks like Della Mornay.'

Although the body was covered with mud, she could see the marks on the girl's arms. They were the same as the marks on Karen's body.

'You shouldn't have released Marlow,' Otley said. 'He probably did this one too.'

'I had to let him go. If Shefford hadn't made so many mistakes at the beginning of the investigation –'

'Don't you talk about my boss like that!' Otley shouted. 'He was a good policeman. He knew Marlow was the killer. He thought he'd done another murder in Oldham –'

'What? Why didn't you tell me?'

'He wasn't certain.'

'There must be reports on this other case. I want them on my desk tomorrow morning. And Otley – if you hide any more information from me, I'll have you moved to another department.'

Chapter 5   Della Mornay's Diary

Peter Rawlings was cooking dinner when Jane telephoned him.

'Sorry, love,' she said. 'I won't be coming home tonight. We've found another body.'

He knew that she must be exhausted. She had not slept for more than thirty-six hours. At the same time, he was annoyed. She had no time to spend with him. She never had time to talk about *his* work or *his* problems. He was having a difficult time at work and he missed Joey, his son. He wanted to talk to Jane but she was never there.

Tennison stood up from her desk. She had been sitting for hours and she was stiff and tired.

She went into Otley's office to see if he was still there. Maybe she could speak to him and persuade him to stop working against her.

Otley wasn't there.

On his desk there were some photographs of Shefford and his family. Next to them were the case notes on Della Mornay. She opened the file. Underneath a pile of papers, there was a small book, a diary for 1989 with Della's name written on the front page. Nobody had told Tennison they had found a diary. She looked through it. Some pages were missing.

It was so late when Tennison got home that she did not want to wake Peter. She slept in the other bedroom. Peter found her there in the morning, lying across the bed. He took her a cup of coffee.

'Jane . . . Jane!'

'What? . . . What?'

'Hey, it's OK, it's me. I brought you some coffee.'

'What time is it?'

'Just after six-thirty. I have to go.'

'Oh no! I have to hurry! I have to . . .' She fell back on the pillows. 'I'm so tired.'

'What time will you be home tonight?' Peter asked.

'Don't ask me.'

'I am asking you. I've hardly seen you for three days. I thought we might go out somewhere for dinner.'

It was the last thing she wanted to think about. Still half asleep, she drank her coffee.

'I'll try to be home by eight, OK?' she said.

Tennison took Jones with her when she went to look at the body. The smell of the body made her feel sick. Jones took one look then had to leave the room.

'She has similar wounds to the other victim,' the doctor said. 'She was killed with a small, sharp knife or tool. Deep cuts to her chest and shoulders. Her face was badly beaten. Marks on her arms show that she was tied up. The hands were washed. She must have fought the person who attacked her – she had false nails and two of them are broken.'

'Do you think the same man killed her?' Tennison asked.

'I can't be certain, but it is possible. Whoever it was, he cleaned the body well and left no evidence of himself.'

Tennison found Jones sitting outside the door. He looked very pale.

'OK,' she said cheerfully. 'If you're feeling better, you can drive me back to the station.'

'Sorry about that, boss,' Jones replied. 'I must have eaten something last night that made me ill.'

Tennison smiled.

At nine o'clock George Marlow left his house and went to the factory where he worked. He did not see the two policemen who followed him.

Marlow worked for a company which made paint. His job was to sell the paint to shops and he often travelled across the country on business trips which took him away from home for two or three days. He was good at his job, he worked hard and his colleagues respected him. They knew that he had been to prison, but he said he wasn't guilty and they believed him.

That morning, nobody spoke to Marlow when he went into the factory. Later in the day, it got worse. When he walked into a room, people turned away. They knew the police had arrested him for murder. They might believe that he was innocent once, but not twice.

Late that afternoon, Marlow wrote a letter.

'I'm leaving this job,' he wrote. 'I cannot work in a place where people suspect me.'

As he walked out of the factory he shouted, 'I didn't do it! I didn't do it!'

♦

Tennison was talking to the officers on the case.

'She died about six weeks ago. Like Karen, she was killed somewhere else and then taken to the field. She was tied up like Karen. What have you found out, Muddyman?'

'Marlow went to work today, but he's left his job. He travels a lot.'

'Where was he at the beginning of December?'

'He was in London.'

'Right, so we know he was in London when both murders took place. Have we found Marlow's car yet?'

'No. None of his neighbours have seen it for about two weeks.'

'Keep searching for it,' Tennison said. 'And check out the area where the second body was found. See if anyone saw a car like his. It's an unusual model. Somebody must have seen it.'

After the meeting, she went to see Kernan. Otley was with him.

'I want to ask Sergeant Otley a question, sir,' Tennison said. 'How well did D C I Shefford know Della Mornay?'

'He'd arrested her a few times,' Otley said. 'She used to give him information.'

'If he knew her, why did he think the body of Karen Howard was Della Mornay?'

'Her face was almost destroyed. Anyone can make a mistake . . .'

'What is this about?' Kernan asked.

'I want to know how well Shefford and Otley knew Della Mornay. And I want to know why this,' she threw the diary on Kernan's desk, 'was in Otley's desk.'

Otley did not reply.

'There are pages missing,' Tennison said. 'What was in those pages?'

'The dates when Shefford went to see her. He liked her – he was one of her customers,' Otley said. He did not look at Tennison as he spoke.

Tennison turned to Kernan. 'I still think Marlow is our prime suspect. I want him watched all the time. If he's killed twice, he could kill again.'

Kernan nodded and she continued. 'I also want to talk to the newspapers and television about this case, sir.'

She had won, and she knew it. She walked out and left them there, closing the door quietly behind her.

There was a moment's silence then Kernan shouted, 'You fool! You've destroyed evidence. You could lose your job for that!'

'I only tore out the pages which had John's name on them, sir,' Otley said. He stared at the floor. He could not look at Kernan.

'You've been lucky this time. Tennison could have finished you.'

Jane arrived home late at night. Peter was waiting for her.

'I thought we were going out tonight,' he said.

'I forgot. I'm sorry, I meant to phone you but there's so much happening at the station.'

The telephone rang. 'If that's another call for you to go back to work,' Peter said, 'I shall leave you!'

Jane picked up the telephone. The call was from her mother.

'It's your father's birthday next Monday and I'm organising a party,' her mother said.

'We'll be there,' Jane replied.

After she put the telephone down, she remembered.

'Oh no! Next Monday I'm appearing on television to ask for information about Karen Howard's murder. It's one of those crime programmes. It's really important – I'm the first female police officer they've asked to go on television.'

'Which is more important, Jane?' Peter asked. 'This case or your father's birthday?'

Jane did not answer.

♦

Moyra stood at the bedroom window. She could see the police officers outside watching the house.

'Why won't they leave us alone?' she asked. She began to cry. 'I just want them to leave us alone.'

'They will. I promise you Moyra, I didn't do this murder. They'll have to leave us alone.'

'Why did you have sex with that girl in the first place?' Moyra asked.

'I don't know. I was stupid. It won't happen again, I promise. I love you, Moyra.'

Chapter 6   Work – and Family

Jane Tennison was nervous as she waited in the television studio. The programme was going to start soon. She knew what she had to do but she was frightened of making a mistake. She was the first woman police officer to appear on a television crime programme and she had to do well.

Jane's parents, her sister Pam and Peter were watching the

television, waiting for the programme to begin. The birthday party had started earlier, but they wanted Jane to arrive before they cut the birthday cake.

'Peter,' Jane's mother said, 'can you check the video? Jane wants us to record the programme so that she can watch it later.'

'Is the video on the right programme, Mr Tennison?' Peter asked.

'Of course it is. Now be quiet so we can watch.'

Otley sat with the other police officers who were watching the programme. He hated seeing Tennison on television.

Tennison was doing well.

'We know that Karen Howard left the office where she was working at six-thirty on the evening of the thirteenth of January. She told the people she worked with that she was going home. She never returned to her apartment. Were you in Ladbroke Grove that night, at around six-thirty? Did you see her?'

A woman police officer, dressed in the same clothes as Karen had worn, appeared on the screen.

'We know that Karen had problems starting her car. A man saw her trying to start it.'

On the television, a man went over to the girl dressed as Karen.

'Got a problem?'

'Yes. It won't start.'

The man tried to help but still the car would not move. He shook his head. 'I think you'd better call a garage.'

'We know that Karen locked her car and walked to the main road. She was never seen again,' Tennison went on.

George Marlow stood in front of the television watching the programme.

'Turn it off!' Moyra said. 'What are you watching that for?'

'Because I want to see what she's saying. Somebody out there knows what happened – they know who killed her.'

'The police think it was you.'

'Well, it wasn't. You have to believe me.'

Moyra watched the television with horror as a car like George's appeared on the screen. Tennison was saying that the police needed to find the car as part of the investigation.

'George!' she screamed. 'They've got a car like yours! They're giving out the car number!'

Marlow put his head in his hands. 'Why are they doing this to me? Why?'

After the programme finished, Jane drove quickly to her parents' home. She had forgotten to send her father a birthday card and present, so she bought two bottles of wine from the shop near their house.

'Well, was I OK?' she asked. 'Did you see me on television? Have you recorded it on the video? Switch it on – let me see myself.'

Peter switched on the video. Jane sat on the edge of her chair. The television showed a football match.

'What's this? You've recorded the wrong programme!' Then she began to shout at her father.

There were only ten phone calls to the police station after the programme finished. One of them was useful. A woman called Helen Masters remembered seeing Karen getting into a car. She gave a description of the driver. He was about five feet ten inches tall, rather handsome, with very dark hair. She described George Marlow.

Jane and Peter argued all the way home.

'Your father just made a mistake,' Peter said. 'He didn't record the wrong programme on purpose.'

'He knew how important it was. He always gets it wrong!'

'You are so selfish! Don't you ever think about anyone except yourself? It was your father's birthday and all you could do was shout at him.'

'It's always the same. They don't care about my job. They think I should be like Pam and have children ...' Suddenly Jane began to laugh. 'He's done this before, you know. He recorded part of a football match over the video of Pam's wedding.'

When she opened the door to the apartment, the telephone was ringing. 'We've got a witness,' she said to Peter. 'A woman saw Karen get into a man's car. She says the man knew Karen – he called out her name. And he looked like George Marlow. I'm going to question him again.'

'Tonight? You're going back to the station now?'

Quickly, Jane changed her clothes, kissed Peter and left the apartment. Peter lay back on the bed and sighed. Sometimes she really annoyed him – her moods, her temper.

Chapter 7   A Witness

Helen Masters was a good witness.

'I was standing near the railway station,' she said. 'I saw the man first. He had dark hair . . . Then I saw the girl. I recognised her later when I saw her photograph on television. The man walked to the edge of the pavement and called to her.'

'You definitely heard him call her name?' Tennison asked.

'Oh yes.'

Helen Masters was asked to identify the man she had seen.

Twelve men stood in a row. Each man held a number in front of his chest. George Marlow was number ten.

Helen looked at them through a window. She could see them but they could not see her. Each man was asked to step forward and shout the name 'Karen'. Eight . . . nine . . . ten.

Looking straight ahead, George Marlow called out 'Karen' loudly. Helen Masters stared at him for a long time.

The reception area of the police station was busy. Tennison thanked Helen Masters for her help, even though she wanted to scream with anger. Helen had not identified Marlow as the man she had seen.

Marlow left the station with his lawyer, Arnold Upcher. As he walked past Tennison, he stopped.

'Why are you doing this to me?' he asked. 'I was pulled out of bed at four o'clock this morning. You have a policeman following me all the time. You know I'm innocent. Why are you doing this?'

'Get him out of here,' Tennison said.

Maureen Havers came up to her.

'Kernan wants to see you.'

'Tell him you couldn't find me.'

'Marlow's lawyer is with him. He says you shouldn't have given out the number of Marlow's car on television last night. You could only do that if the car was reported stolen, and Marlow hadn't reported it.'

'Oh no! Well, do something about it. We all know that reports of stolen cars can get lost. The report has probably been put in the wrong drawer, hasn't it?' Maureen nodded and smiled.

Tennison and Jones went to the factory where Marlow had worked to talk to his boss.

'Has George always worked in London?' Tennison asked.

'He started work in Manchester. We moved the factory to London in 1982. George still travelled around the Manchester area – he knew all the customers.'

'Did anyone go with him?'

'Moyra always went with him. She had family up there.'

'I need a list of all the places he visited.' Tennison said.

Later that day at a meeting of all the policemen working on the case, Otley told them what was happening.

'These photographs show the bodies of Karen and Della. You can see that the marks on their bodies are the same. We know that the DNA tests show Marlow had sex with Karen before she died, but he has explained that. He also has a reason why Karen's blood was on his coat — he says she cut herself on his car radio. We have nothing to link him with Della Mornay. I think his car is important. We've still not found it, but if we do, there may be enough evidence in it to prove he did the murders. So find the car!'

Tennison came into the room.

'Karen didn't fight when she was attacked. Her fingernails were short and clean and there was no blood on them. They had been cleaned with some sort of brush. Della did fight. Her fingernails were long and false and she lost three of them.'

'Did Marlow have any scratches on his body when we searched him?' Burkin asked.

'No he didn't,' Tennison replied. 'We have no evidence to prove that he killed Della or that he went to her apartment with Karen's body. But I still think he's the murderer.'

Otley went to see Kernan.

'We're not making progress,' he said 'She's making a mess of this case.'

'Let her continue,' Kernan said. 'We can't get rid of her unless there's a good reason. The best thing you can do is try to co-operate with her.'

'I miss Shefford,' Otley said. 'He was a good policeman and he was my friend.'

'We all miss him, Bill. But you have to work with Tennison whether you want to or not.'

As Otley left Kernan's office, he met Maureen Havers. She

was carrying a pile of reports on murders in the north of England, in places which Marlow had visited.

Otley helped her carry the papers.

'If you find anything in Oldham, Maureen, let me look at it first.'

'OK,' Maureen said.

Chapter 8   Connecting Evidence

Maureen Havers complained to Sergeant Otley. It was the third Sunday she had worked and she did not like it. She put a pile of boxes on the desk.

'It's Sunday. I should be at home with my family, not working.'

'Have you found any murders reported in Oldham?'

Maureen pointed at his desk. 'The file is on there.'

Burkin ran into the room. He had a newspaper in his hand.

'Look at this,' he said.

Jane Tennison was at home. She hated cooking but she had promised to make a meal for Peter's friends the following night. Her sister Pam was helping her to plan the menu. The sisters were very different. Jane had no patience with house-work; Pam loved it. She had married soon after she had left school and had two children. Her third child was due in the next two weeks.

Peter came into the room carrying a newspaper.

'Look at this,' he said. On the front page of the newspaper was an interview with Marlow.

'I'm innocent,' the story in the newspaper said, 'but the police are following me and making me look like a criminal.'

There was a picture of Tennison and some other officers on the case.

'That's spoiled everything,' Jane said. 'We can't ask witnesses to identify Marlow when they've seen his picture in the newspapers. And these photographs show which officers are following him.'

She picked up her coat. 'I'm going to the police station.'

In the interview room, someone had pinned a copy of the newspaper on the wall. Angrily, Tennison tore it down.

'OK,' she said. 'We've all seen the newspapers.'

Otley smiled. 'Some of them say that women police officers shouldn't be in charge of murder cases like this.'

Before Tennison could reply, Maureen came in.

'Kernan wants to talk to you,' she said.

Otley told the officers to start work again. 'We have a list of murders which took place in the north of England. I want you to check for any that happened when Marlow was in the area.'

'Have you finished looking at the Oldham reports?' Maureen asked him.

'Not yet,' Otley replied.

He had looked through some of them and he knew there was a problem. He was not certain what to do next.

When Tennison came back she told them what Kernan had said.

'Marlow is no longer being followed officially, so I want four officers to watch him without Kernan knowing.'

'What else did Kernan say?' Burkin asked.

'If I don't get some evidence against Marlow soon, I'm being moved off the case,' she said quietly.

The officers worked all day and late into the night.

'We have several cases which we need to look at,' Otley told Tennison. 'Murders in Oldham, Southport and Warrington.'

'Make a list of the officers who are available and send them up to investigate. See if there is any connection with Marlow,' she said.

After Otley left, Maureen Havers asked, 'Why is Otley so interested in Oldham? Does he have family up there?'

'What do you mean?' Tennison said.

'Well, he asked me for the reports on murders in Oldham and now he's said he wants to go up there tomorrow.'

Slowly, Tennison realised what Maureen was saying.

'Let me look at the Oldham reports.'

There was one case which interested her. Jeannie Sharpe, aged twenty one, a prostitute, murdered in 1984. The head of the investigation was . . . Detective John Shefford.

Why was Otley so interested in this case? It had to be connected with Shefford. She decided that she would go to Oldham tomorrow, not Otley.

♦

'Good morning,' Jane said to Peter as he came into the kitchen.

'Where were you last night?' he asked

'I came in late so I slept in the other bedroom. I didn't want to wake you.' Peter did not reply.

'I'll come home as early as I can tonight,' Tennison said. 'I haven't forgotten your friends are coming for dinner. I'll be in Oldham all day.'

She ran out of the apartment.

Peter stood looking at the door.

'Oldham? That's two hundred miles away!'

When they arrived in Oldham, Tennison and Jones were met by Sergeant Tomlins. He told Tennison and Jones about the murder of Jeannie Sharpe. 'She was found in an empty building,' he said. 'She was tied, her face was badly cut, clothes torn off.'

'It's a nasty place to die,' Tennison said.

'Well, these prostitutes ask for it!'

'She was only twenty-one years old, sergeant,' Tennison replied angrily, but Tomlins was already walking away.

'You can talk to some of her friends,' he said. 'They're all prostitutes too. We try to clean them off the streets but they're like rats – they keep coming back.'

The apartment was cold and damp, but somebody had tried to make it look cheerful. Tennison was sitting in an old chair beside a table on which there were two full ashtrays. She was talking to two of the dead girl's friends, Carol and Linda. Carol, a badly dressed but attractive woman in her thirties, was telling her about the last time she had seen Jeannie alive.

'We came out of the pub. There was a car parked near the corner of the street.'

'What sort of car?' Tennison asked.

'A dark one,' Linda said. 'I think it was dark and it had a lot of silver on the front. Anyway, the driver called out to Jeannie . . .'

'He called out? You mean he knew her name?'

'I don't think he called her name, just asked her how much. She went over and got into the car. We never saw her again.'

Tennison showed them the newspaper photograph of Marlow. 'Was this him?'

'I don't know. He had dark hair but I didn't see his face.'

'The police who were working on the case were horrible,' Carol said. 'There was one – Shefford was his name – they got rid of him.'

'Why?' Tennison asked.

'I suppose they found out about him and Jeannie,' Carol said. 'He was one of her customers. He said he'd look after her.'

'Poor kid,' Linda said. 'She had a bad life. Then she ended up tied up and dead in some empty building.'

♦

It was late. Peter checked his watch. He was waiting for Jane to come home.

The front door crashed open and Jane ran in.

'I'm sorry! We were late getting back from Oldham. Don't worry – the meal will be ready before your friends arrive.'

She was right. When Peter's friends arrived, dinner was ready.

Two hours later, they were still sitting at the table finishing the wine. Jane was bored and she had drunk too much. The three men were talking about their work and their wives only talked about clothes.

'Peter told me you work for the police,' Sue said. 'What do you do? Are you a secretary?'

'No,' Tennison said. 'At the moment I'm investigating a murder.'

'I think some women ask for trouble,' Lisa said.

'What, ask to be murdered?' Jane asked.

'Not exactly, but . . .'

'Nobody asks to be murdered,' Tennison said angrily. 'It could happen to you.'

The telephone rang and Jane went to answer it. As she left the room, she heard Peter say, 'Sorry about that.'

'Don't apologise for me,' Jane shouted. 'I can speak for myself.'

After the guests had gone, Jane said, 'Well, I think they enjoyed themselves.'

'Do you?' Peter asked. 'Did you have to start talking about those women and your case?'

'Why shouldn't I?'

'Because it's always you, Jane. Your job, your life. You, you, you! You don't care about anybody else.'

'That's not true!'

'You care about your officers, your victims, your prostitutes. You give all your time to them.'

'That's my job!'

'Tonight was for *my* job and *my* friends, but you still have to take over.' Suddenly Jane felt very tired, too tired to argue.

'Look,' she said, 'I'm sorry. I drank too much wine, and those people were so boring . . .'

'Do you ever think how boring you are when you talk about work all the time? How many times have we talked about George Marlow? Do you know how boring that is for me?'

'Peter, I've said I'm sorry.' She began to cry. She cried for the girls she had seen that day, the prostitutes whose lives were so sad and so dangerous.

Peter knelt down beside her. 'I'm sorry, love. Let's go to bed. We'll talk tomorrow.'

Jane went to bed but she could not sleep. Next morning when she got up the kitchen was still full of dirty dishes and food as it had been the night before. She put on her coat.

'I've been thinking, Peter,' she said. 'I love you, but you're right. I put my work first. It *is* more important to me than anything else. I don't think I can change because I'm doing what I always wanted to do. I have to put everything into my work . . .'

She was telling him that she could never be the sort of woman he wanted.

Somebody knocked at the door. 'That'll be my car,' she said. 'You'd better go.'

'I don't know what time I'll be home tonight.'

'Peter, I've said I'm sorry.' She began to cry.

Peter stood in the kitchen after she left, looking at the dirty dishes, then he reached out and knocked them all to the floor.

♦

Tennison sat silently next to Jones as he drove. Finally he spoke to break the silence.

'Are you OK?'

'I want Marlow's car found,' Tennison said.

'Trouble at home? My wife was angry when I was so late getting home. My dinner was burned.'

'The difference is that you get your dinner cooked for you. I have to cook as well as everything else.'

Kernan had come in early to talk about the Marlow case. He stood and watched as Tennison and Otley shouted at each other.

'George Marlow was questioned in 1984 about the murder of a prostitute called Jeannie Sharpe. John Shefford was one of the officers on the case. He was moved to London because it was discovered that he was having a relationship with the murdered girl,' Tennison said. 'None of this has been put in the files. We now know that he was having a relationship with Della Mornay. He must have known that he identified the wrong girl. He was hiding something.'

Otley was very angry. 'That's a lie. If John Shefford was alive . . .'

'He's not alive, he's dead, and now you're protecting him. You requested the Oldham reports because you knew Shefford was involved . . .'

'That's not true!'

Kernan interrupted. 'That's enough! Calm down, both of you!'

'Sir,' Tennison said. 'I've been working as hard as I can to solve this case. George Marlow is still my only suspect for both of the London murders and a possible suspect for the murder of Jeannie Sharpe.'

'I don't know anything about Jeannie Sharpe's murder,' Otley said. 'I know some of the officers are friendly with these girls . . .'

'Friendly!'

Kernan banged his hand on the desk.

'Be quiet! Did Shefford think there was a connection between the first murder and Jeannie Sharpe?'

'I don't know,' Otley replied. 'I wanted to check the case. When I read the report, I saw John's name. I wanted to see what it was about.'

Kernan nodded, then said, 'You've got work to do. You can go now.'

Otley hesitated. It was obvious Kernan wanted to talk to Tennison by herself. He turned to her.

'Maybe we got off to a bad start,' he said. 'I was upset by John's death. Maybe I should have taken a holiday . . .'

She nodded.

After he had gone, Kernan said, 'What do you want to do?'

'I want Otley taken off this case and I want an officer I worked with before brought in. Detective Amson. He's a good man. And I want Marlow watched all the time.'

Kernan nodded. He knew that this was the price he must pay to hide the mistakes which Shefford and Otley had made.

As Tennison crossed the car park Otley came over to her.

'Look, I'm sorry,' he said. 'I think we started badly. Would you like to come for a drink so we can talk?'

Tennison shook her head. 'Has Kernan spoken to you?'

Otley shook his head.

'No. Look, I didn't know about John working on the Jeannie Sharpe case . . .'

'Yes, you did,' Tennison said quietly. 'You're off the case, Bill.

I've brought in someone else. And I want the names of all the officers on this case who have been friendly with prostitutes.'

Otley stared back at her but there was no anger left in him. She gave him a small nod and walked towards a car that had just come into the car park. It was driven by the new detective, Terry Amson.

'Glad I'm back working with you,' he said. 'How's it going?'

Tennison smiled. 'I think I'm doing OK.'

Otley's sad figure was still standing there as they drove away.

Chapter 9 More Information

Terry Amson drove up the motorway. He and Tennison were going to talk to the woman Marlow had attacked before he was sent to prison. Tennison told Amson what had happened in the case up to that time.

'We have three girls, Della Mornay, Karen Howard and Jeannie Sharpe. All of them were tied in the same way. I still think Marlow is the man.'

Pauline Gilling lived in a small house with her father. It took her a long time to open the door because it had so many locks.

She was about thirty-eight but she looked older. She spoke in a soft voice as she told them about the night Marlow attacked her.

'It was the seventh of November, 1988, about four-thirty in the afternoon. I worked in a flower shop, but it was closed for the afternoon. I went to the hairdresser's.'

She was very nervous and kept coughing as she forced herself to speak. 'As I came up to the front door, I heard somebody call my name. "Pauline! Hello, Pauline!" I turned round and saw this man. I didn't recognise him. He was smiling and he walked towards me. "Aren't you going to invite me in for a cup of tea, Pauline?" I said I was sorry, I thought he'd mistaken me for somebody else. Then he came very close and grabbed me by the throat and started pushing me into the house. He kept hitting me and I fell down, then he kicked me.'

She stopped speaking.

After a moment, Tennison said, 'And then your father came in?'

'Yes. He was upstairs. Daddy called my name and the man ran away. My father is blind. He couldn't identify the man.'

'But you were able to identify him?'

'Oh yes,' Pauline said. 'He was clever, he had a beard when he attacked me but he shaved it off afterwards. But I recognised his eyes. I'll never forget his eyes . . . If my father hadn't called out, George Marlow would have killed me.'

Tennison crossed the room and sat beside Pauline Gilling. 'Thank you for telling me what happened. I'm sorry you had to talk about it again.'

'I think about it all the time,' Pauline said. 'Every time someone knocks at the door or there's a strange sound at night, I expect him to come back and kill me. I had to leave my job. I can't sleep. He should have been in prison for years but they let him go after eighteen months. I'm frightened that he'll come back. He said he would.'

As Tennison climbed back into the car, she said to Amson, 'Marlow had a beard when he attacked her and then shaved it off! That matches what the girls in Oldham told me. They thought that Jeannie's murderer had a beard.'

♦

Two men were painting the row of garages near Marlow's house. A few yards away, Marlow stood, his hands in his pockets, watching them.

One of the men went to his van for another tin of paint.

'Excuse me, are you painting all of the garages?' Marlow asked.

'Just these,' Detective Lillie said.

'Most of the people around here park on the road,' Marlow went on. 'My car was stolen from here not long ago. It was a beautiful car, a Rover Mark III, about twenty years old. I loved that car. It had all these silver badges on the front.'

He continued talking as the two policemen went on painting.

Late in the afternoon Tennison and Amson visited Brixton Prison. They wanted to talk to Reginald McKinney who had been a prisoner with Marlow.

'You were in prison with Marlow, weren't you?'

'That's right.'

'And you met him again after you were both released from prison?' Tennison asked.

'Yeah. I met him in London. We went for a meal and then he drove me home. I offered to take the train but he said he was driving near my house because he wanted to do some work on his car at his garage.'

Tennison was careful not to show how excited she was. 'He had a garage?'

'Yeah. That car was really important to him. He spent a lot of time on it.'

A prison guard looked round the door.

'There's a telephone call for DC Tennison.'

Tennison took the call. The officers had found reports on two more bodies in the north of England which had marks on them like those of Karen Howard and Della Mornay.

♦

Marlow was still talking to Rosper and Lillie when the police cars arrived.

Tennison jumped out of the first car. She ran up to Muddyman.

'Marlow has a garage in another area of London. Search his flat for the keys. They must be somewhere.'

Marlow watched them running towards his house.

'I don't believe they're doing this,' he said.

Moyra cried as she looked at the damage. The police had rolled back the carpets and removed the floor, they had moved all the furniture and even looked inside the toilet. Tennison and Amson examined all the keys they had found.

'Why are you doing this?' Moyra shouted. 'You've searched the place before. Put everything back where it should be!'

Tennison turned to Marlow.

'You know what we're looking for, George. Why don't you tell us where the keys are?'

'I park my car out on the street. I don't have a garage.'

'Your car isn't always on the street. We've asked the neighbours.'

'When it's not parked there I'm away on business.'

'George,' Tennison said, 'we know you have a garage. A friend of yours told us.'

'What friend? I don't have any friends because of you! Now you've made people think I'm a murderer . . .'

'We have a witness who says you told him you have a garage . . .'

'Was it someone I was in prison with? Let me guess. It was Reg McKinney wasn't it?' Marlow laughed. 'You must be desperate if you believe him. He's crazy. He and I had an argument – he's no friend of mine.'

There was a knock on the door and Amson came in.

'Nothing,' he said. 'We haven't found any keys.'

In a low voice, Marlow said, 'I don't have a garage. If I had, maybe I would still have my car.'

Amson drove Tennison home. She was pleased to have a friend working with her. She knew that she could talk to Amson, that he was on her side.

'If he's hidden his car, we'll find it,' Amson said.

'What do you think of Marlow?'

'If he's lying, then he's very good at it.'

'Yes,' Tennison said with a sigh. 'For the first time tonight I doubted that he's the murderer. What about Shefford?'

'As a suspect? He was one of the best police officers I've ever met.'

'He was also in the area when Karen, Della and Jeannie were killed. We're going to have to check him out. I want you to look through all his files tomorrow. And don't tell anyone what you're doing.'

Jane reached for the light switch. The apartment was quiet. She put down her bag and took off her coat, shouting 'Peter? Pete?'

There was no answer. She opened the kitchen door. The room was clean and tidy. The bedroom was the same.

She opened the cupboard to put her coat away. One half of it was empty. She checked all the cupboards and drawers – all Peter's clothes were missing!

In the bathroom there was only one toothbrush and one towel. As she stood by the door, the telephone rang. She picked up the phone. Next to it was a letter.

'Jane, it's Mum. Your sister Pam has just had a baby, a little girl . . .'

'Hello Mum,' Jane said as she tore open the envelope.

The letter contained only one piece of paper.

'I listened to what you said this morning. I can't live with you or your work. I'm sorry to leave you like this but I think it will be best for both of us. I still love you, but I can't see a future for our relationship. Maybe in a few weeks we can meet and talk.'

♦

As she drove to the hospital to see Pam, she wondered if all her relationships would end like this. Peter was not the first man who had left her because she didn't have enough time. She'd never been able to stay with a man for more than a few months.

She parked the car and looked at herself in the mirror. She looked terrible. Her hair needed washing and she needed fresh make-up.

It was late and there were only a few visitors in the hospital. A nurse told her which room to go to. When she reached the door she looked through the window and saw Pam holding the new baby. Pam's husband Tony sat with his arm around her shoulders. Their two other children were sitting on the bed.

Watching them, Jane's hand tightened on the door handle. They looked like a perfect family, a family to which she did not belong.

She turned away and walked slowly back down the corridor.

Later she went back. When she went into the room Pam wasn't there but the baby lay in its bed. Jane moved the blanket to look more closely at the baby's face.

Pam came back and they talked until a nurse came in and said that it was time for Jane to leave.

'Give my love to Peter,' Pam said.

'If I see him I will. It's finished.'

Pam was upset. 'Oh no! Why? Is there someone else?'

'No, there's no one else. We both agreed that it was better to finish it.'

'Well,' Pam said, 'you know what you're doing. Have you solved that case we saw on television?'

Jane paused before she answered. Her family did not understand anything about her work. They did not understand her or how she felt about Peter leaving.

'No, I haven't got him – yet. Goodnight. I'll see you again soon.'

As she closed the door only the expression in Jane's eyes showed how lonely she felt. Now all she wanted was to go home and cry.

Chapter 10   Maureen's Idea

'What do you think you've been doing?' Kernan demanded.

'We had good reason to search Marlow's apartment . . .'

'I'm not talking about Marlow! Why has Amson been looking through Shefford's files? Are you so desperate to find a murderer that you're accusing him?'

'I talked to Amson last night . . .'

'Leave it, Jane! There's no evidence that Shefford was involved.'

'I'm sorry, but I think . . .'

He did not let her finish.

'You've been all over the country trying to find evidence against one of the best officers I've ever worked with. I'm bringing in Chief Detective Officer Hickock to take over. As soon as he arrives, you're off the case.'

Amson came running down towards her as she left Kernan's office.

'We've found another murder that links with the others. It happened in Blackburn in 1987. That means there's been one murder every year except for the time Marlow was in prison. Everyone is waiting for you in the meeting room.'

'What about Shefford?' Tennison asked. 'Did he investigate this murder as well?'

'No.'

'Good,' Tennison said.

At least thirty people were waiting for her. Some of them were drinking coffee and eating sandwiches; the rest were talking. The noise was very loud.

Burkin and two other officers came in after Tennison. They had been upstairs with the superintendent.

'What happened?' Muddyman asked.

'We got into trouble for being too friendly with some of the prostitutes. Only a warning this time. I think Tennison gave us some support. Maybe she's not so bad after all. Have you heard? They're saying that Hickock might be taking over the case.'

'Quiet, please,' Tennison shouted. 'Now, we need to look at this case again. Perhaps we've missed something.'

Amson switched on a video which showed the bodies of the girls who had been murdered.

'Karen Howard, the first victim. Her body was found in Della Mornay's apartment and mistaken for her. Look at the marks on her arms. The next victim was Della Mornay. She was killed about six weeks before Karen and her body was hidden in a field. Look at the marks on her arms – almost the same as those on Karen's body. Jeannie Sharpe, killed in Oldham in 1984. Again, note the marks and cuts. Angela Simpson, murdered in a park in 1985.' He showed a picture of a pretty young girl. 'She was a hairdresser. She was getting married. Marlow was interviewed during the investigation. He was staying in a hotel fifty yards away from the park where Angela was found. There were no marks on her arms, but look at this.'

He showed a photograph of Angela's body. 'The knot in the rope which tied her hands is the same as the others. The fifth girl was Sharon Reed. She was sixteen, still at school. She worked part-time in a beauty shop . . .'

When he finished they stopped for lunch. The men continued discussing the case as they ate their meal. Burkin was talking to Muddyman.

'I've been following Marlow for weeks. He's a friendly man, he talks to us every day. Just because he was in the area when the murders happened doesn't mean that he's guilty.'

'We know he lied about the garage, though,' Amson said.

'Yeah, but we only have the word of Reginald McKinney about that.'

Someone called for Tennison. Kernan wanted to speak to her.

'Looks like the boss is going to be taken off the case,' Burkin said.

Maureen Havers found Tennison hiding in the ladies toilet.

'Is Hickock a big, red-haired man? He's in with the commander and Kernan. They're looking for you.'

'Then they'll have to find me,' Tennison said.

She went back to the meeting room to continue talking to the men.

'Right! We now have six victims but no real connection between them. They didn't know each other. They didn't look like each other, they were different ages, had different jobs. The only link is that Marlow was in the area when they were murdered. Did he kill all six? Have we missed something, another link?'

Muddyman waved to get Tennison's attention.

'A witness said they heard a man call out Karen's name. The

same with Jeannie. The woman who was attacked, Pauline Gilling, she said the man knew her name . . .'

'I see what you mean,' Amson said. 'How did he know their names?'

Havers pushed to the front of the crowd. She put up her hand as if she wanted to say something, then lowered it again. She moved closer and touched Tennison's arm.

'Boss . . . this may be crazy but . . .'

'Anything might help,' Tennison said. 'What have you got?'

'There is a connection between the others.'

'To Marlow?'

'No, to Moyra Henson. When I questioned Moyra she said she didn't have a job. About fifteen years ago she was arrested as a prostitute and then she said she worked as a beautician. If she worked when she travelled with Marlow, then perhaps he met the girls through her . . .'

'Good for you!' Tennison said. 'We'll check it out.'

Jones came in carrying some papers.

'This might be useful, boss. I've checked Marlow's address. He's lived in this house for three years. Before that he lived near St Pancras Station. He's had his car for twelve years. He might have a garage near his old house.'

The phone rang. Muddyman answered it. 'Boss? You're wanted upstairs. Shall I tell them you're here?'

'No! Go and bring Moyra in.'

Moyra was not happy at being taken to the station.

'What do you want this time?' she shouted.

Marlow followed her out of the house. 'Do you want me as well?'

Tennison got out of her car. 'Not this time, George.'

They left him standing there, trying to understand what was happening.

53

Tennison checked that Kernan had left the station, then went to interview Moyra.

'I am Chief Detective Officer Tennison. Thank you for agreeing to answer our questions . . .'

'I didn't agree. You made me,' Moyra interrupted.

Tennison opened a file. 'You came here on the sixteenth of January, is that correct?'

'If you say so.'

'You said that you didn't have a job.'

'Yes. What's that got to do with anything?'

Tennison took out another sheet of paper. 'In 1975 we interviewed you. You said then that you were a beautician.'

'So?'

'Were you also a hairdresser?'

Moyra was getting annoyed. 'No.'

'But you are a beautician?'

'Yeah! I do people's faces, hands, nails. You could do with some help,' she said nastily.

'I want to know where you were on these dates.' Tennison listed the dates of the murders.

'I don't know!' Moyra shouted.

'They were dates when George travelled to Warrington, Oldham, Burnley, Rochdale . . .'

Moyra looked up. 'Oh, in that case I was with him. I always travel with him.'

'So on those dates you were with George? Were you working as well?'

'Yes, sometimes. I work in beauty shops when I'm in those places.'

'I want a list of all your customers,' Tennison said.

Half an hour later, Moyra was beginning to look tired.

'I've made a list of all my customers. They come to me to have their nails painted.'

'What do you mean?' Tennison asked.

Moyra showed her own hands. 'See, my nails look real but they're not. The false nail is painted on.'

'Interesting,' Tennison said. 'Did you do Pauline Gilling's nails?'

'I don't know,' Moyra replied. 'I have a lot of customers, I can't remember all their names.'

'Surely you'd remember Pauline. She's the woman George was sent to prison for attacking.' Tennison pushed a photograph of Pauline across the table.

Moyra refused to look at the picture.

'No! She lied. George didn't do anything to her.'

'What about Della Mornay? Was she your customer?' Tennison pushed another photograph across.

'No!'

'Look at her, Moyra. Della Mornay.'

'I don't know her.'

'No? You said that George came home on the night of the thirteenth of January at ten thirty . . .'

Moyra began to fight back. 'Look, I've had enough. Either you let me go home or I want my lawyer here.'

'Where is George's car, Moyra? We know he has a garage. Where is it? We'll find it, Moyra. It's just a question of time.'

Tennison stood up.

'OK, you can go now, but I'll want to talk to you again.'

It was morning when Moyra got home. George made her a cup of coffee.

'What did she want to know?' he asked.

'What do you think?' Moyra asked. She went into the bedroom and took off her blouse and skirt. Marlow followed her.

'What happened at the police station?'

'They asked me about Pauline Gilling. They kept asking me

55

about her. I've supported you, George, but if I find out you've been lying to me . . .'

'I've never lied to you, Moyra. You know that.' He reached out to touch her but she pushed his hand away.

'Where's the car, George?'

'It was stolen. I don't know where it is.'

'It wasn't here, George. You came home that night without it. I remember because your hair was wet and you said it was raining.' She turned and looked at him. 'Is it in the garage? They're going to get you because of that car. If the police find it they can make sure that they "find" evidence in it. They want to get you.'

♦

'Boss! Some new photographs of Karen have arrived.'

Tennison turned away from the mirror where she had been brushing her hair. 'I'm on my way.'

'Everybody is waiting for you in the meeting room. And . . . Kernan is there.'

Tennison looked worried. 'OK.'

When she went into the meeting room, Kernan was standing in the middle of the officers. The moment she entered the room everybody stopped talking.

'You wanted to see me, sir?'

'Just for a few minutes.' Kernan pointed to the door and told Amson to carry on.

'This was on my desk when I came in,' Kernan said, handing her a sheet of paper. 'The officers on your team have supported you one hundred per cent. They all signed this paper to say that they don't want Hickock to take over. Did you know about this?'

Every single man on the team had signed. Tennison's eyes filled with tears.

'No . . . No, I didn't.'

'You're lucky.'

'Luck had nothing to do with it, sir. We've worked hard together on this case.'

He smiled. 'Let me have any new information straight away.'

Tennison went back into the room. The men were listening to Maureen Havers.

'These photographs were taken on the day Karen died. You can see that her nails were short. But these photographs were taken a week before. Look at her fingernails.'

The nails were long and red.

Amson turned to Jones. 'Speak to her friends at the apartment. Find out where she went to have her nails painted.'

All the officers turned to examine the photographs. None of them looked at Tennison. Very embarrassed, she walked to the centre of the room.

'I just want to say how grateful I am for what you did, for supporting me . . .' Muddyman ran in, interrupting her. 'The suspect and his girlfriend are leaving their house, boss.'

Jones came back to Tennison. He had spoken to Karen's friend on the telephone. 'Karen had her nails done at a shop in Covent Garden.'

'Get down there,' Amson said. 'Take Rosper with you.'

'OK, let's go,' Tennison said. 'Amson, you come with me.'

In a moment the room was empty except for Maureen Havers. She looked at the photographs of Karen Howard. She had a beautiful face, young and innocent.

The most important thing to Maureen and everyone else on the team was to catch the murderer before another girl died.

Chapter 11   The Garage

As her car moved quickly through the traffic, Tennison listened to the reports on the car radio.

Detective Oakhill reported George Marlow's and Moyra Henson's movements. 'The suspect is leaving the taxi with Henson. They're going into Great Portland Street Station. Now they've separated. She's gone down to the trains and he's coming out of the north side of the station.'

Haskins interrupted. 'I can see him! I'm following him. He's getting into another taxi . . .'

'We'll go straight to Euston Station,' Tennison said. 'See if we can find him there.'

George Marlow leaned in at the taxi window to speak to the driver and pointed towards Euston, but when he got into the taxi it turned left towards Camden Town.

A car moved in behind the taxi and followed it. Muddyman reported back on the radio.

'We're following him. He's turned back towards Euston Road.'

The black taxi drove down a narrow street and reached the corner of Euston Road. The traffic was heavy and the taxi slowed down. Marlow immediately jumped out and ran into a shop.

'This is Muddyman. Marlow's left the taxi; it is now empty. Repeat, the taxi is empty.'

A young man on a bicycle slowed down by the side of the pavement. He spoke quietly into a radio.

'I've got him. He's going down Euston Road again.'

On the opposite side of the road, Muddyman had left the police car and was following on foot.

◆

*George Marlow leaned in at the taxi window to speak
to the driver.*

Oakhill nearly lost Moyra Henson in the station, but he managed to get on the same train before the doors closed.

He walked through the train until he was standing close to her. Moyra was staring out of the window of the train. She did not know that Oakhill was following her.

◆

Amson looked at a map. 'He could be heading for Euston Station or King's Cross Station . . .'

'Just a minute,' Tennison said. A message came through on the radio.

'Marlow's jumped on a bus . . . no, he's jumped off it again . . . he's behind King's Cross Station . . .'

'There are garages behind the station,' Amson said.

The voice came over the radio again. 'Suspect has gone into a cafe . . .'

'What's he doing?' Tennison asked angrily.

◆

DC Jones was checking out the beauty shops where Moyra had worked. He spoke to the owner of one shop and showed her a picture of Karen Howard.

'Have you ever done this girl's nails?'

The woman looked at the picture and shook her head. 'I don't know. I do lots of people . . .'

'Look at her again. She was found murdered on the fourteenth of January.'

'January? I wasn't here in January. I was on holiday and my friend was working here.'

'What's the name and address of your friend?' Jones asked.

◆

The café was very small. George Marlow stood at the counter drinking coffee. When the only other customer in the café left, Marlow spoke to the owner.

'Can I have the keys, Stav?'

Stavros pulled a box out from beneath the counter. 'I haven't seen you for a while, John,' he said. 'Have you been away?

'Yeah,' Marlow said. 'How much do I owe you?'

◆

Moyra Henson changed trains twice and finally came out at Oxford Street. With Oakhill following her, she walked from one shop to the next, looking through windows at the clothes and shoes.

◆

A message came through to Tennison from Jones.

'I've found the shop where Moyra was working in January. Karen used to come here to get her nails painted. And when Moyra worked here, Marlow used to meet her after she finished. If Moyra did Karen's nails, Marlow could have seen her when he came to the shop, and found out her name . . .'

'Did you hear that?' Tennison asked Amson. 'George could have found out all the girls' names if they were customers of Moyra's.'

'So she knew what he was doing?'

'Looks like it.'

Tennison told Oakhill to arrest Moyra and take her back to the police station.

Another message came through. 'I've got Marlow! He's just passed me. He's walking towards the garages on Battle Bridge Road . . .'

'Yes!' Tennison shouted. 'He's going to the garages. I knew it!

I knew it!' She gave her orders over the radio. 'Everybody stay back. Don't frighten him. Stay where you are until we're ready to get him.'

The team closed in around Marlow. He did not see them, did not realise that the mechanic bending over an old car, the man on the bicycle carrying a ladder, the two people in the van which drove past, were all police officers.

George Marlow reached the corner of the road where it ran beneath the railway lines. He paused, looking around carefully to see if anybody was following him.

'Don't move,' Tennison instructed over the radio. 'Let him get inside the garage before you grab him.'

Marlow walked slowly, turning the key around his finger. He approached a garage which looked as if nobody had used it for years.

Tennison's voice was quiet. 'I want him to use the keys, everybody wait . . . wait . . .'

After another long look around, Marlow chose one key and put it in the lock of the garage door.

'He's going in!' Muddyman whispered. 'He's opening the door.'

The door opened and Marlow stepped inside. Tennison shouted, 'Go! Go! Go!'

Police cars screamed into the street. Rosper, Caplan, Lillie and Muddyman ran from their hiding places and surrounded Marlow. Rosper, the first there, grabbed him by the shoulders, almost tearing the coat off him as he dragged him from the door. All the officers wanted to get Marlow and they handled him roughly.

Tennison's car arrived. She was about to get out when she hesitated, to give the officers a chance to finish the arrest. At that moment, for no more than a few seconds, she saw another side to the character of her suspect.

Marlow seemed unconcerned at being arrested. In fact, he was unnaturally calm. He looked at Rosper and Lillie, and Tennison could see by the expression on his face that he was angry with himself.

'You . . . the painter near my house!'

He had not suspected they were police officers; he had trusted them. He had been foolish, made a mistake. That was why he was angry.

♦

Moyra Henson came out of a clothes shop carrying a large bag. Oakhill and Woman Police Officer Southill came up behind her.

'Moyra Henson, I would like you to come with us to the police station . . .'

Moyra swung her bag to hit Southill in the face then kicked at her, screaming that she wanted to be left alone. Her screams echoed down the street. Suddenly she stopped and put her hands over her face.

'Please leave me alone! I just want to be left alone. Don't touch me. I'll come with you, just don't touch me.'

She allowed herself to be led to the waiting police car.

♦

The garage was very big. Water came through the roof forming pools on the floor. The far end was dark. Near the centre of the garage was a large, covered shape.

'Watch where you stand,' Tennison ordered. 'Are there any lights?'

Someone switched on the lights. Tennison approached the middle of the room. She raised the covers.

'Well, we've got the car! There's no radio in it. I want this car checked over for evidence.'

Amson was walking towards her. She stepped back, knocking in to him. As she turned to tell him to be careful, she looked past him to the far end of the garage.

'Oh, God,' she whispered. 'This is where he did it.'

On the wall were heavy chains and a collection of sharpened tools and knives.

♦

'Who will you question first?' Kernan asked Tennison.

'Moyra. She was lying when she said Marlow was with her on the night Karen was murdered.'

'Right, Jane, and . . . well done!'

'Not done yet,' she replied. 'Not yet.'

Moyra sat smoking a cigarette. Her lawyer was beside her. Tennison could feel the change in her; Moyra was afraid.

Tennison spoke to Moyra's lawyer. 'Mr Shrapnel? You know that we haven't arrested Moyra yet, but she's agreed to help us by answering some questions.' The lawyer nodded.

For the first time since entering the room, Tennison looked straight at Moyra.

'At twelve forty-five today, we entered George Marlow's garage in King's Cross. We found a brown Rover car there. When I spoke to you last, you said you didn't know where the car was. Is that true?'

'I didn't know anything,' Moyra said. 'I thought it was stolen.'

'You also said that George came home at ten-thirty on the night of the thirteenth of January.'

Moyra nodded.

'When I interviewed you, you said that you didn't know any of the girls who were murdered.' She put down a picture of Della Mornay. 'You and Della Mornay were in court together in 1971, charged with prostitution.'

'You and Della Mornay were in court together in 1971.'

Moyra did not react. Tennison put down another photograph.

'Karen Howard was a customer at the shop in Covent Garden where you worked in January.'

Tennison put down two more photographs.

'Moyra, look at these. If you don't want to look at Della, then look at Karen. George called out to her, offered to take her home in his car. He took her back to the garage and he murdered her. But first he cut her and beat her and tied her body to chains on the wall. *Look at her, Moyra!*'

Slowly Moyra picked up the photographs. She stared at each one, then covered the one of Karen's body with her hands.

'Would you get the men to leave, just the women stay . . . I won't talk in front of them.'

Amson led Shrapnel out of the room. Moyra began to speak.

'I didn't know Della, I didn't even remember her from 1971. But I did her nails . . . she came in sometimes if one was broken and I fixed it for her.'

Tennison nodded. Moyra did not really want to talk about Della, that was not why she wanted the men to leave the room. There was something else. Moyra sat forward and spoke very quietly.

'He . . . did it to me once,' she whispered. 'He made this thing . . . with rope and chains to tie me up. It hurt me. He said it made sex better. I didn't like it. I wouldn't do it again.'

She hung her head. 'I didn't know . . . I didn't know. God forgive me, I didn't know . . .'

Moyra put her face in her hands and began to cry.

Amson and Muddyman were leaning against the wall outside the room when Tennison opened the door.

'George Marlow *was* home by ten-thirty that night but he went out again at a quarter to eleven. She doesn't know what time he returned.'

Tennison stood very straight, head up, eyes bright. 'We've got him,' she said quietly.

♦

In the garage at King's Cross, officers examined the car and took photographs. Jones and Burkin were looking inside a cupboard.

'Look at this!' Burkin said. He held up some rubber gloves. They found clothes – shirts, trousers and coats, all clean and wrapped in plastic bags.

The two men examined the floor.

'There's blood here . . . and this looks like skin . . . God, the smell!'

Burkin found a handbag. Inside there was a purse.

'It's Karen Howard's.'

Jones did not understand how it happened. One moment he was doing his job, looking at the evidence, and the next he was crying like a child. He stood there unable to stop the tears streaming down his face.

Burkin put an arm around his shoulders. 'Go and get some coffee, OK?'

'I'm sorry, I'm sorry, I don't know what made me get like this . . .'

'It's OK. We all go through it, Dave,' Burkin said.

♦

Tennison switched on the tape machine and began talking.

'This is Chief Detective Officer Jane Tennison. Also present are Detective Terence Amson and Mr Arnold Upcher. We are in room 5-C at Southampton Row Police Station. The date is Thursday the first of February 1990. The time is 4.45 p.m.'

She nodded to Marlow. 'Please give your full name, address and date of birth.'

He sat forward and spoke into the machine. 'George Arthur Marlow, twenty-one High Grove Estate, Maida Vale. Born in Warrington, 11th September 1951.'

'Do you understand why you are under arrest?'

'I guess so.'

'We have arrested you as a suspect for the murders of Karen Howard and Della Mornay. Do you understand?' Tennison asked.

'I'm not guilty.' Marlow turned and looked at Upcher.

'Please tell me what happened when you met Karen Howard on January thirteenth.'

'I didn't know her name, I was told her name later,' Marlow began. 'She approached me. I asked her how much she wanted. We had sex and I paid her. I didn't know her, I'd never met or seen her before. Then I took her back to the station . . .'

'What about the cut on her hand? You said she cut it on the car radio.'

'Yes, that's right.'

'We now know there is no radio in your car.'

Marlow did not react to her words. 'I was home at ten-thirty . . .'

'What time did you next leave the house?'

'I didn't. I watched television with my wife.'

'Your wife told us that you left the house again at fifteen minutes to eleven. She can't remember when you came back, but you returned without your car. She says that your car wasn't stolen from outside the house.'

'She's wrong! My car was stolen, I never went out again.'

'You say that you didn't know Karen Howard?'

'Yeah, I'd never met her before that night . . .'

'Moyra admits that she knew Karen – she did her nails at a shop in Covent Garden. You were there at the time and spoke to Karen. Is that true?'

'No.' Marlow shook his head.

'You also said you didn't know Della Mornay. Moyra says that you did.'

Marlow sat back in his chair and folded his arms. 'I don't believe you. You must have made Moyra say that. She's scared of you – I'm not!'

The team were waiting in the meeting room. Jones asked, 'How's the boss? She must be exhausted.'

Burkin shook his head. 'It's taking a long time.'

Marlow looked tired. 'How many more times do I have to tell you?'

'What happened this morning?' Tennison asked.

'Somebody called me, didn't give his name. He said he'd seen my car on the television and he knew where it was. At King's Cross.'

'He told you your car was in a garage at King's Cross? You were seen unlocking the doors.'

He answered angrily. 'The man on the phone said I could get the keys from the cafe. I got the keys but I didn't find my car because just as I opened the door, the police jumped on me! I don't know why I have to keep telling you this.'

Tennison showed no sign of impatience as she said, 'The man in the cafe said he rented the garage to a man called John Smith. He also cleaned your clothes for you, didn't he?'

Marlow shook his head. Tennison continued, 'Come on, George, how did you get Karen into Della's apartment? Where are the keys? You knew the place was empty, didn't you? You knew because Della was already dead.'

'I'm not saying any more,' Marlow said. He turned to Upcher. 'Tell her that's enough! I want to go home.'

'That isn't possible, George,' Upcher said quietly.

'I want to see Moyra! I want to go home!' Marlow was getting very angry.

'We can have a fifteen minute break,' Tennison said. 'You can't see Moyra.'

Suddenly Marlow stood up. 'This is a mess, isn't it? All right, I did it.'

Upcher jumped to his feet. Tennison sat and stared at Marlow, then she said, 'Could you repeat that?'

Marlow closed his eyes. She could see every line of his handsome face. He wet his top lip with his tongue, then he opened his eyes. Tennison recorded every movement in her mind.

He put his head to one side. Nobody in the room moved, they all looked at Marlow, at his strange, frightening smile.

'I said I did it.'

There was nothing else to say. Marlow seemed completely comfortable.

Eventually Tennison spoke, 'Please sit down, George.'

She watched him carefully as she asked, 'What did you do?'

He counted his fingers as he spoke the names. 'Karen, Della, Angela, Sharon, Ellen and . . .' He screwed up his eyes, trying to remember, 'and Jeannie. That's right, Jeannie . . .'

George Arthur Marlow had just admitted killing six women.

Chapter 12   Celebrations

After Marlow was taken away, Tennison lit a cigarette. Catching Marlow had exhausted her, taken away from her the man she loved, stopped her sleeping and nearly lost her her job. She sat quietly and smoked her cigarette until it was finished.

Jones ran into the bar of the local pub where the other officers were waiting. 'He's admitted it! All six of them, he's admitted killing them all!'

The team rose to their feet and began cheering. An officer from another police station asked Havers, 'What's going on?'

'Our boss just got a suspect to admit to six murders! Biggest case this station's ever had . . .'

Tennison faced Kernan across his desk.

'Well done,' he said. 'The trial will take a long time, but you go home now and get some sleep. You deserve it.'

'Yeah, I need it. It was a long night.'

The phone rang and Kernan answered it. 'Yes . . . just a minute.'

'You were right,' he said to Tennison. 'The beautician link . . . it was a woman's case after all!'

'Fifty per cent of murder victims are women, so I should have plenty of work to do!' Tennison replied.

'Woman's case!' she said to herself, still angry at Kernan's remark. She saw Maureen Havers.

'Maureen, are any of the officers here?'

'Oh, I think they've gone home,' Havers replied. 'They were all tired – it's been a long day. Jenkins wants the meeting room cleaned out. He asked if you could go down there before you leave.'

The meeting room was full of people. Every member of the team was there. Someone called, 'Here she is!' and they all watched as the handle of the door turned.

Tennison walked in to cheers and whistles. A huge bunch of flowers was put in her arms and Burkin started shouting, 'Three cheers for the boss!'

'I thought you'd all gone home,' Tennison laughed. She bit her lip, but the tears still came. Then she started laughing through her tears.

'We did it! We got him!'

♦

Many months later, George Marlow stood in court as the charges against him were read out.

'George Arthur Marlow, you are accused of murdering Karen Howard on the thirteenth of January 1990 . . .'

Karen's mother and father could not look at him. He had taken their daughter and murdered her; waiting for him to be caught had been the worst part of their lives. Marlow had not only destroyed their daughter, he had destroyed them.

'. . . that on the third of December 1989 you murdered Della Mornay . . .' Two prostitutes, friends of Della's, sat forward to look at the murderer.

'. . . on the fifteenth of March 1984, you murdered Jeannie Sharpe, that in January 1985 you murdered Ellen Harding . . .'

Carol and Linda had travelled down from Oldham. Linda could only see the top of Marlow's head. Jeannie had wanted so much from life but she got nothing, nobody to help her or love her.

Carol twisted her handkerchief in her hands. She could still remember Marlow calling Jeannie's name.

A young man sitting near Carol sat forward and stared at Marlow.

'. . . that in July 1986 you murdered Angela Simpson . . .'

The young man began to cry when he heard Angela's name. The years between Angela's death and the arrest of Marlow had been very hard. For five years he had wondered if perhaps he

Many months later, George Marlow stood in court as the charges against him were read out.

could have saved her. For five years he had lived without the girl he loved and wanted to marry.

'. . . and in October 1987 you murdered Sharon Reed . . .'

Sharon's father sat at the back of the court. Sharon's mother had died three years ago. He had lost his daughter and then his wife. Every day he remembered them . . .

Tennison kept her head down, avoiding looking at Marlow. She looked up suddenly as the door opened and a dark figure walked in. It was Moyra, and she looked twenty years older.

'George Arthur Marlow, you have heard the charges. Are you guilty or not guilty?'

Tennison looked at him. He was very handsome with his dark eyes and shining hair. He looked back at her and as their eyes met, he seemed to smile.

'Not guilty,' he replied.

ACTIVITIES

Chapters 1–5

Before you read

1 Look at the picture on page 3. What do you think has happened? Who do you think the two men are?
2 Check these words in your dictionary:
   arrest DNA evidence investigate
   prime prostitute senior
   Which words match these phrases?
   a someone with a more responsible job than yours
   b proof that someone is guilty of a crime
   c take a crime suspect to a police station and keep them in a cell
   d best; most important
3 Write a sentence using this group of words:
   prostitute/murder/investigate/DNA
4 Find these words in your dictionary:
   charge (v) *fingerprints identify release*
   Write two or three sentences as part of a police report and make sure you use all three words at least once.

After you read

5 What do Shefford and Otley remove from the scene of the crime?
6 Why does Jane Tennison get the Della Mornay case?
7 How does Tennison know the murdered girl is not Della Mornay?
8 Why is Marlow released?

Chapters 6–10

Before you read

9 What do you think will happen to Peter and Jane?
10 If you need an *ashtray*, what are you probably doing?
11 Check the words *badge* and *beautician* in your dictionary.
    Which word could you add to:
    a make-up/nails/skin . . .
    b club/metal/silver/ . . .

After you read

12 Explain why the newspaper report makes the investigation more difficult.

13 Is Peter right to be angry with Jane after the dinner party? Can you understand Jane's point of view? Discuss this with other students.

14 What important ideas do these officers have?
    a Maureen Havers
    b Jones

15 Why does Kernan leave Tennison on the case?

Chapters 11–12

Before you read

16 What do you expect to happen next?

After you read

17 How does Moyra change her evidence?

18 What do the officers find in Marlow's garage?

19 Why do you think Marlow says in court that he is not guilty?

Writing

20 Would you want to work with someone like Jane Tennison? Why or why not?

21 Imagine you are Stavros. Write a report for the police about how you met George Marlow. Explain why you agreed to rent him the garage and clean his clothes. What did you think he was doing?

22 'Prime Suspect shows the problems of a woman working in a man's world.' Does it do so successfully? Give reasons for your answer.

Answers for the Activities in this book are published in our free resource packs for teachers, the Penguin Readers Factsheets, or available on a separate sheet. Please write to your local Pearson Education office or to: Marketing Department, Penguin Longman Publishing, 5 Bentinck Street, London W1M 5RN.